Agnès Couderc

The Amazing Fate of Raoul Raccoon

Little, Brown and Company

Boston Toronto London

There once was a raccoon named Raoul. His parents ran a laundry. They worked and worked and worked, doing the washing for all the animals in the forest.

Raoul, however, did not work. He did not
like laundry. He detested it. He preferred to
lie back and relax, much to his parents'
despair.

"Laundry gives me pimples," he said by
way of an excuse.

But in his way, Raoul was ambitious. All day long, he dreamed of becoming famous like the people he read about in magazines and in his schoolbooks.

One day, he made a big decision.

"Enough!" he said. "I will control my own fate! I'll become a famous sailor!"

So he packed his bag and left his parents a note:
"I love you. Good-bye." And he left forever.

After several days' walk, Raoul came to the seashore. Since Raoul seemed to be a willing worker, a captain hired him as a sailor's helper on his boat, *The Conqueror,* which was about to leave for an expedition to the North Pole.

"What a great adventure!" Raoul said to himself as he climbed aboard.

Everything was going well...until one day, when the captain was busy looking at his charts, and the ship crashed into an iceberg.

The Conqueror sank, and so did Raoul's seagoing career.

"Oh, well, to be a sailor was not really my fate," Raoul thought as he rowed away. "And besides, I was feeling a bit seasick."

Not discouraged, Raoul Raccoon set off to try something else. He joined the air force, and after several weeks, he was ready for his first solo flight as a fighter pilot.

"All right! This is the way to fame and fortune!" he exclaimed before takeoff.

That day, the air force lost one of its best planes because
of someone's slight piloting error.

"I might have confused the ejection button with
the turbo-reactor switch," Raoul said to himself as he
drifted to the ground.

But Raoul was a determined fellow and was still convinced that he would triumph at *something*.

"I'll become a motorcycle racer. I'll win all the big prizes. I'll never, ever have to go back to the laundry."

But during his first race, a fly splattered on Raoul's visor. He couldn't see where he was going, and he lost control.

At this point in his troubled career, Raoul Raccoon decided to change his approach.

"Enough of sports. What I really am is a deep thinker. My fate demands that I devote myself to research."

He set out to discover a magic formula that would make him big, strong, handsome, and, above all, terribly sexy.

"With the help of this potion," he thought, "I'll dazzle Hollywood and become a big star."

Alas, once again, his hopes were dashed.

After fixing the damages caused by his supposedly magic brew, Raoul left research behind and trained to become a policeman in New York City.

"It is my fate to uphold law and order. Robbers beware!"

"Freeze. I've got you surrounded!"

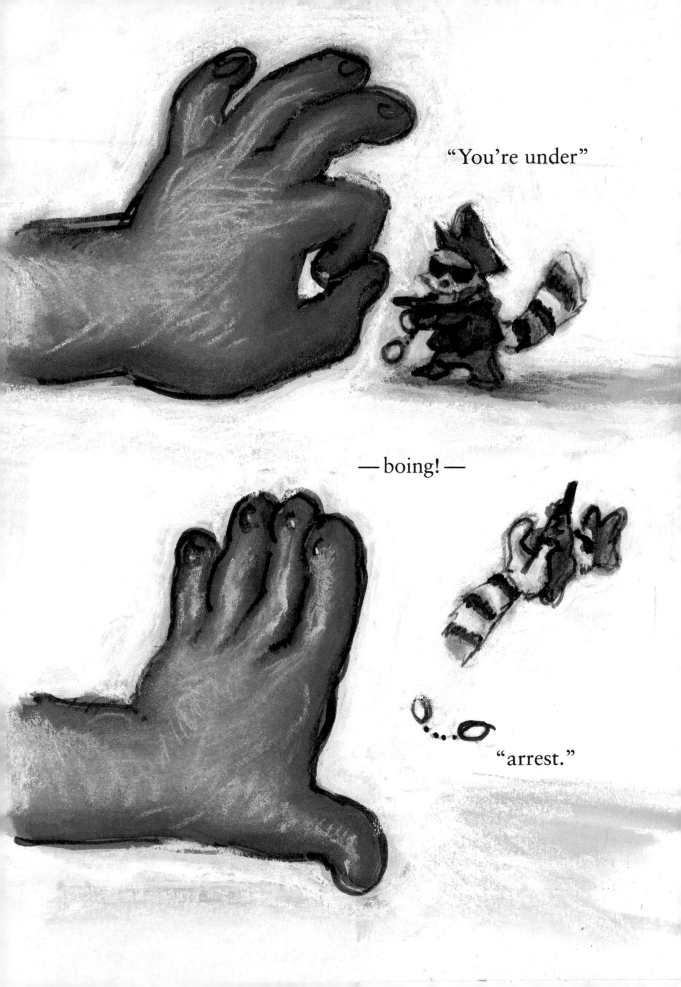

This was the last straw. Poor Raoul was really discouraged.

"I'm sick of this! I'm just a rotten no-talent raccoon. I'm going to end it all. Good-bye, cruel world..."

"You called?" asked a voice behind him.

"Me? I didn't call anyone."

"Yes, you did. You said, 'Good-bye, cruel world.' That's my name: Good Byecruelworld. I'm the good fairy of lost causes. Do you have a wish you'd like to make?"

"I thought my fate would lead me to success. I want to succeed at something, anything!"

"I see. I can help. Now, what were those magic words
again?... Ah, yes!
Arakichna youpla,
No-talento raccoono golo natchda poof!"

At that moment, Raoul, who you remember, had hated laundry, was struck with a brilliant idea. He quickly invented a machine that did laundry all by itself.

He made his fortune and became the president of his own company:
Wonder Wash by Raoul.

Thanks to him, no one in the forest had
to do laundry by hand again.
Raoul's fate had been right in front of him all
the time. Amazing!

First U.S. Edition 1993
First published in France in 1992 by Hachette Jeunesse

Library of Congress Catalog Card Number 92-54541
Library of Congress Cataloging-in-Publication information is available.

10 9 8 7 6 5 4 3 2 1

Printed in France